영어로 읽는 세계명작
Story House

THE THREE LITTLE PIGS

6 아기 돼지 삼형제

Joseph Jacobs

WorldCom Edu

Adapted by **Lori Olcott**
Illustrated by **Shin Yun-Kun**

Copyright © WorldCom Edu 2006

Published in Korea in 2006 by WorldCom Edu

All rights reserved. No part of this publication may be reproduced, stored in a retrieval system, or transmitted in any form or by any means, electronic, mechanical, photocopying, recording, or otherwise, without the prior written permission of the publisher.

Printed and distributed by WorldCom Edu

작가와 작품 설명

조지프 제이콥스(Joseph Jacobs 1854~1916)는 1854년 시드니에서 태어났으나 곧 영국으로 이민을 떠나게 되었다. 그는 뛰어난 고전학자이자 평론가로서 유대인의 역사와 전통에 대한 여러 가지 책을 펴냈으며 지금은 영국의 동화 작가로 널리 알려져 있다.

주요 저서로는 『아기 돼지 삼형제』 외에도 우리에게 잘 알려진 『잭과 콩나무』, 여러 나라의 설화를 수집하여 쓴 『이솝 우화』 등이 있다.

작품 설명

세 마리의 아기 돼지가 엄마 돼지 곁을 떠나 홀로서기를 하면서 겪는 이야기로, 재치있게 문제를 해결하면서 자신들의 행복을 찾는 내용이다. 어린이들에게 형제간의 우애와 성실, 지혜에 관한 훌륭한 교훈을 들려주는 동화로 여러 세대에 걸쳐서 많은 사랑을 받아 왔다. 1843년에 첫 출판되었고 1892년 Joseph Jacobs에 의해 개작되었다.

Introduction

Hello, and thank you for your interest in Worldcom's Story House! I hope you and your children enjoy the stories and characters we present to you here.

These Fairy tales have been passed down from parent to child for generations and generations. They usually teach a lesson. They teach the values that are important in every culture; like being kind, generous and helpful to others. They show that looks can be deceiving. Something beautiful, can be cruel and evil. But something ugly, can be good and loving. They also teach the value of patience. Rewards for good deeds don't always come quickly. But be patient, and the good deeds you do will bring good deeds to you. And if you keep working hard, your efforts will pay off.

I have tried my best to re-tell these stories in modern and natural English, without being too complicated or too hard. Most middle school children can read these stories. But I hope that parents and other adults will enjoy reading these books with their children too. There are interesting parts in each story. I hope there is enough that everyone will enjoy reading the story and listening to the native speakers.

Again, thank you for joining us in Story House. We hope you enjoy your stay.

이 책을 펴내며

안녕하세요. 월드컴의 Story House에 오신 것을 환영합니다. 부디 여러분과 여러분의 자녀들이 이 책이 들려주는 이야기들을 만끽하시길 바랍니다.

이 동화들은 부모에서 아이들에게로 여러 세대에 걸쳐 전해내려 온 이야기로서 교훈을 담고 있습니다. 이웃에게 친절하고 서로 도우면서 아낌없이 베푸는 것, 이러한 가치관의 중요성을 일깨워 주죠. 이러한 것들은 때때로 반대로 표현되기도 합니다. 겉보기에는 아름답지만 잔인하고 사악할 수 있으며, 비록 흉칙하게 보여도 착하고 사랑을 베푸는 사람일 수 있다는 것입니다. 이러한 이야기들은 우리에게 인내의 가치를 일깨워 주기도 합니다. 선한 행동의 대가는 그 즉시 되돌아오지 않습니다. 그러나 참고 기다린다면, 여러분의 선한 행동은 보답을 받을 것입니다. 그리고 열심히 노력한다면 그에 상응하는 결과를 얻을 것입니다.

저는 이 이야기들을 너무 복잡하거나 어렵지 않도록 현대적이고 자연스러운 영어로 전달하기 위해 최선을 다했습니다. 이 책은 중학교 수준의 학생이라면 누구든지 읽을 수 있습니다. 그러나 부모님을 비롯한 모든 이들이 자녀분들과 함께 이 책을 즐길 수 있기를 바랍니다. 이야기마다 제각기 재미있는 부분들이 있습니다. 네이티브들이 들려주는 생생한 이야기는 현장감을 더해 주어 자신도 모르는 사이에 동화세계에 빠져들게 될 것임을 믿어 의심치 않습니다.

다시 한 번 저희 Story House에 오신 것을 감사드리며, 계속 많은 사랑 부탁드립니다.

Lori Olcott

등장인물 ✿ 주요 등장 인물

셋째 돼지
엄마 돼지 곁을 떠나 위험한 세상 속에서 혼자 힘으로
살아가려는 현명하고 부지런한 돼지.

첫째 돼지
돼지 형제의 맏형이지만 게으른 성격과 엄마돼지가
누누히 강조하셨던 말씀을 잊은 채 행동한 탓에 위험에
처하게 된다.

둘째 돼지
혼자 힘으로 살아가려 하지만 놀기 좋아하는 성격 탓에
첫째 돼지와 마찬가지로 위험한 상황에 처한다.

늑대
아기 돼지들을 잡아먹으려고 온갖 꾀를 써 보지만
똑똑한 아기돼지에게 호되게 당하기만 한다.

그 외의 등장 인물

 엄마 돼지

상인들

 놀이 공원 아저씨 외 먹기대회 진행자

Contents

Chapter 4

SH-06-C
MP3

Chapter 1

Once there was a mother pig who had three little pigs. She was so poor, however, that she could no longer take care of the young pigs. So she decided to send them away.

once 옛날에
mother 엄마
pig 돼지
have(-had-had) 가지다
little 조그만, 어린
so ~ that … 너무 ~해서 …

poor 가난한
however 그러나, 하지만
no longer 더 이상 …않다[아니다]
take care of …을 돌보다
decide to …하기로 결심하다
send away 멀리 보내다

She was so poor, however, that she could no longer take care of the young pigs. 하지만 엄마돼지는 너무 가난해서 더 이상 새끼돼지들을 돌볼 수가 없었습니다.

So she decided to send them away.
그래서 엄마돼지는 새끼돼지들을 멀리 보내기로 결심했습니다.

It is time for you to go out into the world now. You are old enough to live on your own. Remember that hard work never hurt a pig. But I warn you, if you are lazy and get fat, then you will be too slow to run away from you know who.

 The hungry old wolf!!

The three pigs were scared and shouted. So the three little pigs left their safe home and went out into the world. They each went a different way, and they each built themselves a new home.

go(-went-gone) out 나가다
into the world 세상으로
enough to …할 만큼의
on one's own 혼자서, 독립하여
remember 기억하다
hard work 힘든 일
never 결코 … 않다
hurt 다치게 하다, 손해를 입히다
warn 경고하다, 훈계하다
if 만약 … 라면
lazy 게으른
get fat 뚱뚱해지다

too ~ to … 너무 ~해서
 …할 수 없다
run away 도망치다
you know who 모두 알고 있는 사람
hungry wolf 배고픈 늑대
scare 두려워하다, 겁먹다
shout 소리치다
leave(-left-left) 떠나다
safe 안전한
different way 다른 길
build(-built-built) 짓다, 세우다
themselves 그들 자신의

You are old enough to live on your own.
너희들은 독립해서 살 수 있을 만큼 나이가 들었어.

Remember that hard work never hurt a pig.
고된 일은 결코 돼지에게 해가 되지 않는다는 것을 명심하거라.

I warn you, if you are lazy and get fat, then you will be too slow
to run away from you know who. 경고하건대 만일 너희들이 게을러서
뚱뚱해지면 몸이 너무 느려져서 너희들도 아는 어떤 이로부터 도망칠 수 없
게 된단다.

The first little pig was very nice and
happy, but he was also very lazy.
He didn't like hard work. He always
looked for the easy way to do things.
Knowing he had to build a house for
himself, the first little pig went to the
market to look for supplies. When he
saw a man selling straw, he said to
himself,

 How easy it would be to build a house
out of straw!

nice 착한
like 좋아하다
hard work 힘든 일
always 항상, 늘
look for …을 찾다
easy way 쉬운 방법
do(-did-done) 하다, 끝내다
things 일
knowing …라는 걸 알고서
have(-had-had) to … 해야만 한다
build a house 집을 짓다

for oneself 스스로, 혼자서
market 시장
supplies (supply의 복수형)물품들
see(-saw-seen) 보다
man 남자
sell 팔다
straw 지푸라기
say(-said-said) to oneself
    (마음 속으로) 혼잣말하다
how 얼마나, 참으로
out of 〈재료〉 …으로

Knowing he had to build a house for himself,
첫째 돼지는 혼자서 집을 지어야 한다는 것을 알고,

How easy it would be to build a house out of straw!
지푸라기로 집을 짓는다면 정말 쉬울 거야!

How much is that straw, sir?

I will sell it to you for two cents, little pig.

I'll take it.

So the first little pig bought the straw, and he built his house.

Well, that was easy. I didn't have to work very hard, and now I have a new house. This is great!

The first little pig went inside and relaxed in his new home.

how much 얼마, 어느 정도	build (-built-built) 짓다, 세우다
sir (존칭)선생님, 나리	easy 쉬운
sell 팔다	work hard 열심히 일하다
cent (화폐 단위)센트	great 멋진, 훌륭한
take 취하다, 얻다	go (-went-gone) inside 들어가다
buy (-bought-bought) 사다	relax 편히 쉬다

I didn't have to work very hard, and now I have a new house.
난 그다지 열심히 일하지도 않았는데 금방 새 집이 생겼네.

Now, the second little pig was a little different from the first. Because he liked to have lots of time to play, he always looked for the fastest way to do things. The second little pig also went to the market in search of supplies for his new house. When he saw a man selling sticks, he said to himself,

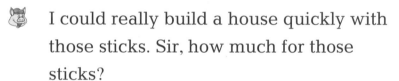 I could really build a house quickly with those sticks. Sir, how much for those sticks?

I will sell them to you for three cents.

Great! I'll buy them.

second 둘째의, 두 번째의	market 시장
different from …와는 다른	in search of …을 찾아서
first 첫째의, 첫 번째의	supplies (supply의 복수형)물품들
because 왜냐하면	stick 막대기
lots of time 많은 시간	say(-said-said) to oneself
look for …을 찾다	(마음 속으로)혼잣말하다
fastest way 가장 빠른 방법	quickly 빨리

Because he liked to have lots of time to play, he always looked
for the fastest way to do things.
둘째 돼지는 많은 시간을 놀고 싶어했기 때문에, 항상 일을 빨리 하는
방법을 찾았습니다.

I could really build a house quickly with those sticks.
이 막대기들이라면 정말 빨리 집을 지을 수가 있을 거야.

So the second little pig bought the sticks
and started to build his house.

 Mom said that we would have to work so
hard, but this is so easy. Look how
quickly I built my house with these sticks.
Now I will have plenty of time to play.

buy (-bought-bought) 사다
start to ···하기 시작하다
build (-built-built) 짓다, 세우다
have to ···해야만 한다
work hard 열심히 일하다

so 매우, 아주
look 보다
how quickly 얼마나 빨리
plenty of time 많은 시간

Look how quickly I built my house with these sticks.
내가 이 막대기들로 얼마나 빨리 집을 지었는지 보라구.

The third little pig was very different from his brothers. He was a very hard worker. He wasn't worried about finding the easiest way or the fastest way. He wanted things done the right way. When he went to market to buy supplies for his house, he looked for something sturdy that would last.

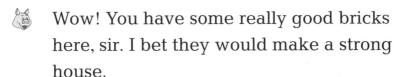 Wow! You have some really good bricks here, sir. I bet they would make a strong house.

These bricks will help you build the finest house money can buy.

How much for all of them?

I will sell them to you for five dollars.

He wanted things done the right way.
셋째 돼지는 모든 일을 올바른 방법으로 끝내기를 원했습니다.

These bricks will help you build the finest house money can buy. 이 벽돌들은 네가 돈으로 살 수 있는 가장 좋은 집을 짓는데 도움이 될 게다.

third 세 번째의, 셋째의
brother 형제
hard worker 부지런한 사람
be worried about
　…에 대해 걱정하다
find 찾다
easiest (easy의 최상급) 가장 쉬운
fastest (fast의 최상급) 가장 빠른
way 방법, 길
do(-did-done) 하다, 끝내다

right 올바른, 맞는
something 어떤 것, 무언가
sturdy 견고한, 튼튼한
last 오래가다, 지속하다
brick 벽돌
bet 확신하다, 장담하다
make …이 되다
strong 튼튼한
finest (fine의 최상급) 가장 좋은
money 돈

Oh, I don't have enough money right now. Can you wait until tomorrow?

 Okay, I will wait until tomorrow, but not any longer.

The third little pig quickly left to find work so that he could earn enough money for the bricks. He worked very hard that day. When he was finished, he had the money he needed.

enough 충분한
right now 지금 당장
wait 기다리다
until …까지
tomorrow 내일
any longer 더 이상
leave(-left-left) 떠나다

work 일, 작업
so that …하기 위하여
earn 벌다
work hard 열심히 일하다
that day 그 날
finish 끝나다, 마치다
need 필요하다

The third little pig quickly left to find work so that he could earn enough money for the bricks. 셋째 돼지는 벽돌을 살 충분한 돈을 벌기 위해서 일거리를 찾아 얼른 떠났습니다.

Early the next morning, he took his
money and bought the bricks, and began
building his house. It took him a long
time, but he knew the bricks would
make his house strong and safe.
When his house was finally
finished, the third pig called
his two brothers over to see
his new home. They came
and admired his work.

early the next morning
다음 날 아침 일찍
take(-took-taken) 가지고 가다
buy(-bought-bought) 사다
brick 벽돌
begin(-began-begun) building
짓기 시작하다
take a long time
오랜 시간이 걸리다

know(-knew-known) 알다
make 만들다
strong 튼튼한, 강한
safe 안전한
finally 마침내, 드디어
call over 부르다
come(-came-come) 오다
admire 감탄하다

but he knew the bricks would make his house strong and safe.
그러나 셋째 돼지는 벽돌로 집을 지으면 튼튼하고 안전한 집이 되리라는
것을 알았습니다.

the third pig called his two brothers over to see his new home.
셋째 돼지는 자신의 새 집을 보여 주려고 두 형들을 불렀습니다.

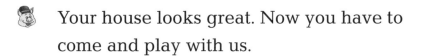 Your house looks great. Now you have to come and play with us.

Yeah! Let's go into the forest to play.

You two go on ahead. I still have some work to do.

Wow, I get tired just WATCHING him work.

Remember, mother pig warned us not to get fat and lazy.

Oh, he is so silly. He loves to work, and he never plays.

So the first little pig and the second little pig went into the forest to play while the third little pig stayed home and worked. What the pigs did not know was that in that same forest there was a scary, smart and very hungry old wolf.

look great 멋있어 보이다
with us 우리와 함께
yeah (yes의 구어적 표현)그래
Let's …하자
go into …로 들어가다
forest 숲
go ahead 먼저 가세요
still 아직도, 여전히
get tired …ing …하는데 지치다
watch 지켜보다
warn 경고하다, 주의하다

get fat 뚱뚱해지다
silly 바보 같은, 어리석은
love to …하는 것을 매우 좋아하다
never 결코 …않다
while …하는 동안
stay home 집에 머물다
same 같은
scary 무서운
smart 영리한
hungry 배고픈

I get tired just WATCHING him work.
난 저 애가 그저 일만 하는 것을 보니 짜증이 나.

Remember, mother pig warned us not to get fat and lazy.
엄마가 뚱뚱해지고 게을러지지 말라고 주의주셨던 것을 명심해.

I True or False

1. Mother Pig said that hard work never hurt a pig.

2. The three little pigs all went the same way.

3. The first little pig liked hard work.

4. The second little pig liked to have lots of time to play.

5. The third little pig had to earn some money.

II Multiple Choice

1. **What will happen to the pigs if they are lazy and get fat?**

   a. They will be too tired to work.

   b. They will be too slow to run away.

   c. They will be too old to live on their own.

2. **Who was you know who?**

   a. The hungry old wolf

   b. The mother pig

   c. The salesman

3. **Where did the three little pigs find supplies to build their houses?**

   a. They found supplies in the market.

   b. They found supplies in the forest.

   c. They found supplies at Mother Pig's house.

4. **Which house cost the most money?**

   a. The straw house cost the most.

   b. The stick house cost the most.

   c. The brick house cost the most.

5. **Who remembered Mother Pig's warning?**

   a. The first little pig did.

   b. The second little pig did.

   c. The third little pig did.

Comprehension

Checkup I

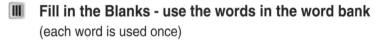

III **Fill in the Blanks - use the words in the word bank**
(each word is used once)

any	build	hard	into	loves
new	plays	quickly	time	wait

1. It is _____ for you to go out _____ the world.

2. I didn't have to work very _____, and now I have a _____ house.

3. I could really _____ a house _____ with those sticks.

4. I will _____ until tomorrow, but not _____ longer.

5. He _____ to work, and he never _____.

정답은 p.118에

IV **Draw a line to connect the first half of each sentence with the second half:**

A

Mother Pig •

The first little pig •

The second little pig •

The third little pig •

The scary old wolf •

B

• built a house out of sticks.

• sent her sons away.

• built a house out of bricks.

• was hungry.

• built a house out of straw.

Chapter 2

The wolf usually ate squirrels, chickens, chipmunks, and other small animals. But today he was hungry for something different. Today he wanted a tender, delicious pig.

 BACON! PORK CHOPS! HAM!
That's what I want for dinner. Wait!!
What is that I smell?
Could it be a tender, delicious pig?

usually 보통, 평상시
eat(-ate-eaten) 먹다
squirrel 다람쥐
chicken 닭(고기)
chipmunk (북미산)다람쥐
other 다른
small 작은
animal 동물
hungry for 간절히 바라는, 열망하는
something 어떤 것

different 다른
tender 부드러운
delicious 맛있는
bacon 베이컨
pork chop 돼지갈비
ham 햄
dinner 저녁 식사
wait 잠깐(만)
smell 냄새맡다

But today he was hungry for something different.
하지만 오늘 늑대는 뭔가 다른 것을 간절히 바라고 있었습니다.

That's what I want for dinner. 그게 바로 내가 원하는 저녁 식사야.

Just then, the scary, smart and very hungry wolf saw the two little pigs playing. He was a sneaky wolf and decided to try to join in their game.

Hello, little pigs. I am a friendly wolf and would like to play with you.

I... I... I don't think so.

Yeah, our mother warned us about you.

The two little pigs stopped what they were doing and quickly ran back to their homes. The wolf followed them and came to the first little pig's house.

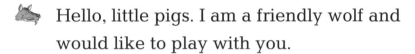

He was a sneaky wolf and decided to try to join in their game.
그는 교활한 늑대여서 돼지들의 놀이에 끼어들기로 마음먹었습니다.

The two little pigs stopped what they were doing and quickly ran back to their homes. 두 돼지 형제는 하던 것을 멈추고 재빨리 각자의 집으로 뛰어갔습니다.

just then 바로 그 때
scary 무서운
smart 영리한
hungry 배고픈
wolf 늑대
see(-saw-seen) 보다
sneaky 비열한, 교활한
decide to … 하기로 결심하다
try to … 하려고 하다
join 참여하다

friendly 친절한, 다정한
would like to … 하고 싶다
think 생각하다
warn 경고하다, 주의하다
stop 멈추다
quickly 재빨리
run(-ran-run) back 뛰어 돌아가다
follow 뒤따라가다
come(-came-come) to
　　… 에 다다르다

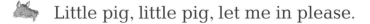 Little pig, little pig, let me in please.

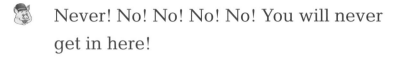 Never! No! No! No! No! You will never get in here!

 Then I will huff, and I will puff, and I will BLOW your house down!!

So the wolf huffed, and he puffed, and he blew the house down.

let in 들여보내다	then 그러면
please 제발, 부디	huff 입김을 내뿜다, 가쁘게 숨쉬다
never 절대 … 않다	puff 훅 불다, 입김을 내뿜다
get in 들어오다	blow (-blew-blown) down
here 여기	불어서 쓰러뜨리다

Let me in please. 제발 날 들여보내 줘.

So the wolf huffed, and he puffed, and he blew the house down.
그리곤 늑대는 입김을 내뿜어 훅 불고는 집을 날려 버렸습니다.

The first little pig was so afraid. He ran as fast as he could to the second little pig's house and began banging on the door.

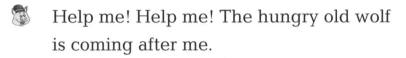 Help me! Help me! The hungry old wolf is coming after me.

Come inside, brother pig. We will be safe in my house.

Shortly after the first little pig was safely inside, they heard a knock on the door.

afraid 무서운, 두려운
run(-ran-run) 달리다
as fast as one could
  가능한 한 빨리
begin(-began-begun) 시작하다
bang 세게 두드리다[치다]
help 돕다

come after …을 따라오다
inside 안으로
safe 안전한
shortly after …한 직후에
hear(-heard-heard) 듣다
knock 두드리다

He ran as fast as he could to the second little pig's house and
began banging on the door. 첫째 돼지는 가능한 한 빨리 둘째
돼지집으로 뛰어가서 문을 두드리기 시작했습니다.

Little pigs, little pigs, let me in. It's the nice wolf.

Never! No! No! No! No! We will never let you in!

Then I will huff, and I will puff, and I will BLOW your house down!!

So the wolf huffed, and he puffed, and he blew the house down.

let in 들여보내다

nice 착한, 마음씨가 고운

then 그리고는, 그러면

huff 입김을 내뿜다, 가쁘게 숨쉬다

puff 훅 불다, 입김을 내뿜다

blow (-blew-blown) down
  불어서 쓰러뜨리다

house 집

so 그래서

We will never let you in! 우린 절대로 널 들여보내지 않을 거야!

Then I will huff, and I will puff, and I will BLOW your house
down!! 그렇다면 내가 입김을 훅 불어서 네 집을 날려 버리겠어!!

The two little pigs were really afraid now.
They ran as fast as they could to the third
little pig's house, so the wolf would not
eat them.

Little brother! Little brother! Help us!
The wolf is trying to eat us.

I thought this would happen. Come into
my house. Hurry!

No, little brother. We should run away.
The hungry old wolf will blow this house
down!

He isn't going to blow MY house down.
It's made of bricks.

The two little pigs went inside the third
little pig's house, and moments later, they
heard a knock on the door.

really 정말로	come into ···에 들어가다[오다]
afraid 두려운, 무서운	hurry 서두르다
as fast as one could	run(-ran-run) away 달아나다
가능한 한 빨리	be going to ··· 할 것이다
eat 먹다	be made of ···로 만들어지다
try to ··· 하려고 하다	brick 벽돌
think(-thought-thought)	go(-went-gone) inside 들어가다
생각하다	moments later 잠시 후에
happen 일어나다, 발생하다	

They ran as fast as they could to the third little pig's house,
so the wolf would not eat them.
첫째와 둘째 돼지는 늑대가 그들을 잡아먹지 못하도록 최대한 빨리 막내
돼지집으로 달려갔습니다.

Little pigs, little pigs, let me come in. It's the nice wolf.

Never! No! No! No! No! We will never let you in!

Then I will huff, and I will puff, and I will BLOW your house down.

let …하게 하다   then 그렇다면

come in 들어가다   blow (-blew-blown) down

nice 착한, 마음씨가 고운   불어서 쓰러뜨리다

Let me come in. 날 들여보내 줘.

We will never let you in! 우린 절대로 널 들여보내지 않을 거야!

So the wolf huffed and puffed and huffed and puffed, but he just couldn't blow the house down! The three pigs cheered, and the wolf went home without a delicious pig in his stomach.

 I must have those pigs to eat. I will have to think of a new plan. I am a smart wolf, and I will just go back to their house tomorrow and trick them.

---

just 단지, 오직
cheer 환호하다
go(-went-gone) home
　집에 가다
without … 없이
delicious 맛있는
stomach 배, 위
eat 먹다

think of …을 생각해 내다
new 새로운
plan 계획
smart 영리한
go back to …로 되돌아가다
tomorrow 내일
trick 속이다

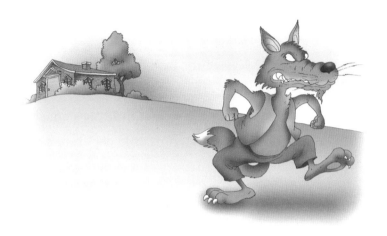

The wolf went home without a delicious pig in his stomach.
늑대는 뱃속에 맛있는 돼지로 배를 채우지도 못하고 집으로 돌아갔습니다.

I must have those pigs to eat. 저 돼지들을 꼭 잡아먹고 말 거야.

I will have to think of a new plan. 새로운 계획을 짜내야겠어.

Comprehension

Checkup II

I **True or False**

1. The wolf wanted roast beef for dinner.
2. The two little pigs let the wolf join their game.
3. The wolf blew down the first little pig's house.
4. The wolf blew down the second little pig's house.
5. The wolf blew down the third little pig's house.

II **Multiple Choice**

1. What dZid the wolf usually eat?
   a. He usually ate pigs.
   b. He usually ate small animals.
   c. He usually ate bad children.

2. How did the wolf first find the little pigs?
   a. He saw them.
   b. He heard them.
   c. He smelled them.

정답은 p.119에

3. **Where did the first little pig run?**

    a. He ran to the second little pig's house.

    b. He ran to the third little pig's house.

    c. He ran to Mother Pig's house.

4. **Where did the first and second little pigs run?**

    a. They ran to the market.

    b. They ran to the wolf's house.

    c. They ran to the third little pig's house.

5. **Why wasn't the third little pig afraid?**

    a. Because his house was made of bricks.

    b. Because the wolf was tired.

    c. Because his brothers were with him.

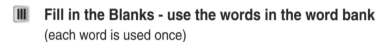

Comprehension

Checkup II

III **Fill in the Blanks - use the words in the word bank**
(each word is used once)

about	different	eat	house	hungry
mother	new	safe	think	wolf

1. But today, he was _____ for something _____.

2. Our _____ warned us _____ you.

3. We will be _____ in my _____.

4. The _____ is trying to _____ us.

5. I will have to _____ of a _____ plan.

정답은 p.119에

IV Draw a line to connect the first half of each sentence with the second half:

<table>
<tr><td align="center">A</td><td align="center">B</td></tr>
</table>

Little pig, little pig, • • get in here.

You will never • • and the wolf went home.

So the wolf huffed, • • let me in please.
and he puffed,

The three pigs cheered, • • and trick them.

I will go back to their • • and he blew the house house tomorrow down.

SH-06-C
MP3

Chapter 3

The next day, he went back to the third little pig's house with a really big, friendly smile.

 Little pigs. You are so smart. You are much smarter than me. I am sorry I tried to hurt you. Let's be buddies. I know a really good field with lots of carrots. Do you want to go with me?

with a really big, friendly smile.
정말 다정하고 큰 함박웃음을 지으며

You are much smarter than me.
너희들은 나보다 훨씬 똑똑하지.

next day 다음 날
really 정말로
big 큰, 커다란
friendly 다정한, 친한
smile 미소, 웃음
much 훨씬(비교급을 강조)
~er than …보다 더 ~한
sorry 미안한, 후회하는

try to …하려고 하다
hurt 다치게 하다
Let's …하자
buddies (buddy의 복수형) 친구들
field 밭
lots of 많은
carrot 당근
go with …와 함께 가다

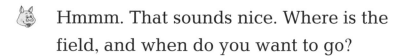 Hmmm. That sounds nice. Where is the field, and when do you want to go?

The field is very close. It's on the side of Farmer Jack's barn. I will come back tomorrow at six in the morning.

When the wolf left, the first little pig and the second little pig turned to their brother and said,

Are you crazy? He is going to eat you!

He doesn't want to eat carrots, he wants to eat you!

The wolf will have to find me first. Don't worry. Just wait and see.

The wolf will have to find me first.
늑대는 먼저 날 찾아야만 할 거야.

Don't worry. Just wait and see.
걱정 마. 그저 두고 보면 알아.

sound …처럼 들리다
nice 멋진, 괜찮은
where 어디에
field 밭, 들판
when 언제
close 가까운
on the side of …의 편에
farmer 농부
barn 헛간
come back 돌아오다

tomorrow 내일
morning 아침
leave(-left-left) 떠나다
turn to …으로 돌리다[향하다]
crazy 미친, 제정신이 아닌
find 찾다, 발견하다
first 먼저, 우선
worry 걱정하다
just 그저, 단지
wait 기다리다

That night, the wolf was thinking to himself,

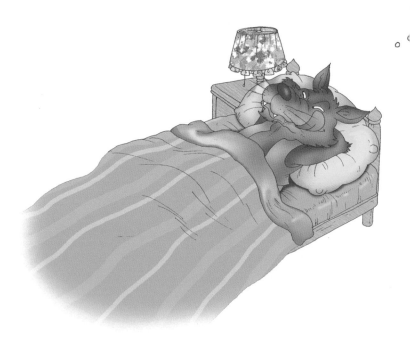

Finally, tomorrow I will be able to eat a tender, delicious pig.

He fell asleep dreaming of pork chops, bacon and ham.

that night 그 날 밤
think to oneself 혼자서 생각하다
finally 마침내, 결국
be able to …할 수 있다
tender 부드러운
delicious 맛있는

fall(-fell-fallen) asleep 잠이 들다
dream of …을 꿈꾸다
pork chop 돼지 갈비
bacon 베이컨
ham 햄

He fell asleep dreaming of pork chops, bacon and ham.
늑대는 돼지 갈비, 베이컨 그리고 햄에 대한 꿈을 꾸면서 잠이 들었습니다.

The next morning at five o'clock, the third little pig got up, so he could get to the carrot field before the wolf.

 Hey guys, come on! Aren't you coming with me?

No way! It's too early, and we're scared.

Okay, I will go by myself then.

next morning 다음 날 아침	guy (구어)사람, 녀석
at five o'clock 5시 정각에	come on (독촉·간청)자, 빨리 빨리
get(-got-gotten) up 일어나다	come with 함께 가다
get to …에 도착하다	No way! 절대 안 돼!
carrot field 당근밭	too 너무 …하다
before …보다 먼저	early 이른
hey (부를 때)어이, 이보게	by oneself 혼자서

The next morning at five o'clock, the third little pig got up, so he could get to the carrot field before the wolf.

셋째 돼지는 늑대보다 먼저 당근밭에 도착하기 위해서 다음 날 아침 5시에 일어났습니다.

The third little pig was not worried at all. He knew what he was doing.
He went to the field and picked carrots then quickly returned home.
At exactly six o'clock, the wolf came to the house and knocked on the door.

 Who's there?

 It's me, Wolfie! Let's go find the carrots now.

not … at all 전혀 … 않다
be worried 걱정하다
know(-knew-known) 알다
go(-went-gone) to …로 가다
pick 캐다, 따다
carrot 당근

return home 집으로 돌아가다
exactly 정확히
knock 두드리다, 노크하다
who's there? 누구세요?
wolfie (wolf의 애칭)늑대

He knew what he was doing.
셋째 돼지는 자신이 무엇을 하고 있는지 알고 있었습니다.

Let's go find the carrots now. 자, 이제 당근을 찾으러 가자.

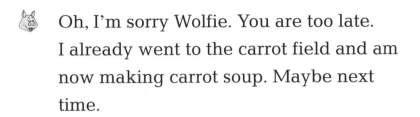

Oh, I'm sorry Wolfie. You are too late. I already went to the carrot field and am now making carrot soup. Maybe next time.

He fooled me this time, but I will get him next time.

So the wolf returned home, and the three little pigs cheered.

All right! He's gone! We tricked him!

Yummmm. That soup sure smells good, little brother. Let's eat!

Sorry guys. No soup for lazy pigs. You have to work for your food.

We should have gone with him to the carrot field.

The third little pig enjoyed his delicious carrot soup all by himself.

late 늦은
already 이미, 벌써
soup 수프, 국물
maybe 아마도
this time 이번에
next time 다음 번에
fool 속이다, 놀리다
get 잡다
cheer 환호하다
all right! 좋았어!, 잘 됐어!

go(-went-gone) 가다
trick 속이다
yum (입맛 다시는 소리) 냠냠
sure 정말로, 확실히
smell 냄새가 나다
lazy 게으른, 나태한
should have … (과거분사)
        … 했어야 했는데
enjoy 즐기다
all by oneself 전부 혼자서

He's gone! 늑대가 갔어!

No soup for lazy pigs. You have to work for your food.
게으른 돼지에게 줄 스프는 없어. 음식을 먹으려면 일을 해야지.

We should have gone with him to the carrot field.
우린 막내와 함께 당근밭에 갔어야 했어.

The next day, the wolf was walking around in the forest, thinking about how he could eat the pigs, when suddenly, an apple dropped on his head.

 Hey, that gives me a good idea.
Pigs really love apples. I will ask them to come with me to the apple orchards.
They won't trick me this time!

The next day, the wolf was walking around in the forest, thinking about how he could eat the pigs.
다음 날 늑대는 어떻게 하면 돼지들을 잡아먹을 수 있을지 생각하면서 숲속을 서성거리고 있었습니다.

I will ask them to come with me to the apple orchards.
사과 과수원에 함께 가자고 돼지들한테 청해 봐야지.

next day 다음 날
walk around 서성거리다
forest 숲
think about …에 대해 생각하다
how 어떻게
suddenly 갑자기
apple 사과
drop on …위에 떨어지다
head 머리

give 주다
idea 생각
really 정말로
love 좋아하다, 사랑하다
ask 묻다, 요청하다
orchard 과수원
trick 속이다
won't (=will not) …이 아닐 것이다

The hungry old wolf went back to the pigs' house.

Hey, I'm not mad at you, pigs. Please come with me tomorrow to the apple orchards, so we can pick some sweet, red apples together.

Why, thank you, Wolfie. Where can we find these fine apples, and what time should we go?

You can find the apples down at the Merry Orchards. I will pick you up at five o'clock.

Why, thank you, Wolfie.
글쎄, 고마워, 늑대야
I will pick you up at five o'clock!
내가 5시에 너희를 데리러 올게!

hungry 배고픈, 굶주린
go(-went-gone) back to
   … 로 되돌아가다
be mad at … 에게 화가 나다
pick 따다, 캐다
sweet 달콤한
red 빨간
together 함께

why (주저할 때)저, 글쎄
thank you 고맙다
fine 맛있는, 좋은
what time 몇 시에
down 아래에
pick up 데리러 오다[가다]
at five o'clock 5시 정각에

The hungry old wolf returned home, thinking how smart he was to come up with such a wonderful plan. Meanwhile, the pigs were making plans of their own.

 I am going to sleep now, because I am going to get up at four o'clock tomorrow morning. If you want apple pie, you have to come with me this time.

 We'll come! We'll come!

Thinking how smart he was to come up with such a wonderful plan. 늑대는 그런 멋진 계획을 생각해 낸 자신을 정말 똑똑하다고 여기고 있었습니다.

We'll come. 우리도 갈게.

return home 집에 돌아가다
think 생각하다
how 얼마나, 참으로
come up with 생각해 내다
such 그런, 이런
wonderful 멋진
plan 계획
meanwhile 한편, 그 동안에
make plans 계획을 세우다

of one's own 자기 자신의
be going to …할 예정이다
sleep 잠자다
because 왜냐하면
get up 일어나다
tomorrow morning 내일 아침
If 만약 … 라면
apple pie 사과 파이
come with …와 함께 가다

The next morning at four o'clock, all the little pigs went to the Merry Orchards. They climbed the trees and began gathering sweet, red apples.

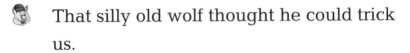 That silly old wolf thought he could trick us.

 Did you ever see anyone so dumb?

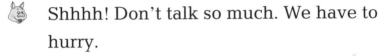 Shhhh! Don't talk so much. We have to hurry.

At that very moment, the wolf ran out from behind a tree.

That silly old wolf thought he could trick us.
그 어리석고 늙은 늑대는 우리를 속였다고 생각했어.

Did you ever see anyone so dumb?
지금까지 그렇게 멍청한 녀석을 본 적이 있니?

next morning 다음 날 아침
orchard 과수원
climb 올라가다
begin(-began-begun) 시작하다
gather 모으다
sweet 달콤한
silly 어리석은, 바보 같은
think(-thought-thought)
  생각하다
trick 속이다

see(-saw-seen) 보다
anyone 어떤 사람, 누군가
dumb 멍청한, 얼간이의
talk 말하다
so much 그렇게 많이
hurry 서두르다
at that very moment
  바로 그 순간에
run(-ran-run) out 달려나오다
from behind tree 나무 뒤에서

Now I've got you! You didn't outsmart me this time.

That's what you think.

The little pigs began throwing apples like bullets and sent the wolf running. The pigs climbed down from the tree and took all their delicious apples home. They baked many apple pies, and this time ALL the pigs enjoyed the food.

This will never be enough pie for me. I could eat a whole mountain of apple pies.

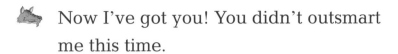

The little pigs began throwing apples like bullets and sent the wolf running. 아기 돼지들은 사과를 총알처럼 내던지기 시작했습니다. 그래서 늑대를 도망가게 만들었습니다.

This will never be enough pie for me. 이 정도의 파이는 내게 결코 충분치가 않아.

get(-got-gotten) …을 잡다
outsmart 속이다, 앞지르다
throw 던지다
like …처럼
bullet 총알
send(-sent-sent)
   내몰다, 억지로 가게 하다
climb down from
   …에서 내려오다
take(-took-taken) 가지고 가다

delicious 맛있는
bake 굽다
many 많은
this time 이번에는
enjoy 즐기다
never 결코 …않다
enough 충분한
eat 먹다
a whole mountain of
   산더미 같은

Comprehension

Checkup III

I **True or False**

1. The wolf wanted to eat carrots.

2. The three little pigs went to the carrot field together.

3. There were sweet, red apples at Merry Orchards.

4. The three little pigs went to the apple orchard together.

5. The three little pigs baked apple pies.

II **Multiple Choice**

1. What was on the side of Farmer Jack's barn?
   a. The third little pig's house
   b. An apple orchard
   c. A carrot field

2. How did the third little pig trick the wolf at the carrot field?
   a. He went there early.
   b. He went there late.
   c. He didn't go to the carrot field.

정답은 p.120에

3. **What did the third little pig do with the carrot soup?**

   a. He gave some to his brothers.

   b. He gave some to the wolf.

   c. He ate it all himself.

4. **What dropped on the wolf's head?**

   a. A carrot dropped on his head.

   b. An apple dropped on his head.

   c. Rain dropped on his head.

5. **What time did the pigs go to pick apples?**

   a. They went at 4:00 in the morning.

   b. They went at 5:00 in the morning.

   c. They went at 6:00 in the morning.

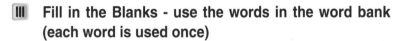

III **Fill in the Blanks - use the words in the word bank (each word is used once)**

able	food	gathering	making	pig
their	trees	when	where	work

1. _____ is the field, and _____ do you want to go?

2. Tomorrow I will be _____ to eat a tender, delicious _____.

3. You have to _____ for your _____.

4. Meanwhile, the pigs were _____ plans of _____ own.

5. They climbed the _____, and began _____ sweet, red apples.

IV **Draw a line to connect the first half of each sentence with the second half:**

A	B

A

B

The wolf went to the pigs house   •

• with me this time.

I know a really good field   •

• with him.

Do you want to go   •

• with lots of carrots.

We should have gone   •

• with a big, friendly smile.

You have to come   •

• with me?

Chapter 4

The next morning while the pigs were out taking a walk, they saw an advertisement that interested them.

Hey brother, look at this! It says there is a Fair going on at the Village Square. Can we go, please?

Oh look! There is a pie eating contest. That's for me!

Well, there are some things I need for the farm. I guess we can go.

they saw an advertisement that interested them.
돼지 형제들은 흥미로운 광고 하나를 보게 되었습니다.

It says there is a Fair going on at the Village Square.
마을 광장에서 박람회가 열린다고 쓰여져 있네.

There are some things I need for the farm.
난 농장에서 쓸 몇 가지 물건이 필요해.

while …하는 동안
out 밖에서
take a walk 산책하다, 거닐다
advertisement 광고
interest 흥미를 끌다
look at …을 보다
say …이라고 쓰여져 있다
fair 박람회
go on (행사 등이)열리다, 치뤄지다

village 마을
square 광장
pie 파이
eating contest 먹기 대회[시합]
things 물건들
need 필요하다, 원하다
farm 농장
guess 추측하다, 짐작하다

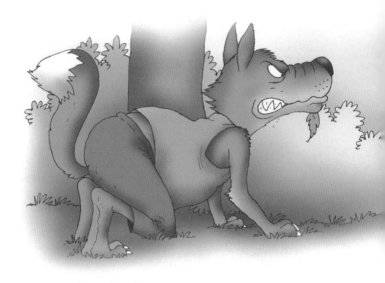

What the pigs did not know was that the hungry old wolf was watching them from a distance. He was up to his old tricks.

 The Fair, eh? I think I'll enter the PIG eating contest rather than the PIE eating contest. This time I'll get there first!

The following day, the pigs were so excited about going to the Fair, they forgot all about the hungry old wolf.

know 알다
hungry 배고픈, 굶주린
watch 지켜보다
from a distance 멀리서
up to …을 꾀하고
old trick 교활한 속임수
enter 참여하다, 들어가다
rather than … 보다는 오히려

get there 그곳에 도착하다
first 먼저
following day 다음 날
be excited about
　　　… 에 기분이 들떠 있다
forget (-forgot-forgotten) about
　　　… 에 대해 잊어 버리다

What the pigs did not know was that the hungry old wolf was watching them from a distance. 돼지들은 멀리서 굶주린 늙은 늑대가 그들을 지켜보고 있다는 사실을 몰랐습니다.

He was up to his old tricks. 그는 교활한 속임수를 꾀하고 있었습니다.

When they arrived, they each wanted to do something different.

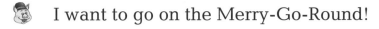 I want to go on the Merry-Go-Round!

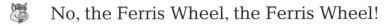 No, the Ferris Wheel, the Ferris Wheel!

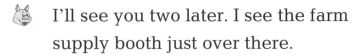 I'll see you two later. I see the farm supply booth just over there.

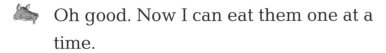 Oh good. Now I can eat them one at a time.

arrive 도착하다
each 각자, 각각
something 어떤 것
different 다른
merry-go-round 회전목마
ferris wheel 회전 관람차
see 보다, 만나다

later 뒤에, 나중에
farm 농장
supply 생활필수품
booth 노점
just over there 바로 저기에
at a time 한번에

When they arrived, they each wanted to do something different.
돼지들이 도착했을 때, 그들은 서로 다른 것을 하고 싶어했습니다.

The wolf immediately put his plan into action. He quietly went over to the Merry-Go-Round and stepped up on the platform, pretending to be one of the horses. The first little pig could hardly wait to ride the Merry-Go-Round. He ran to the man and handed him the money. He jumped on to one of the horses, not knowing he would actually jump on the back of the hungry old wolf!

 Wow! This one has real fur.

The ride started, and suddenly the little pig realized he was not on a Merry-Go-Round horse.

The first little pig could hardly wait to ride the Merry-Go-Round.
첫째 돼지는 회전목마를 타고 싶어서 도저히 기다릴 수가 없었습니다.

not knowing he would actually jump on the back of the hungry old wolf! 첫째 돼지는 실제로 자신이 굶주린 늙은 늑대의 등 위에 올라타리라는 것을 모른 채!

immediately 즉시, 바로
put one's plan into action
  자신의 계획을 실행에 옮기다
quietly 조용히
go(-went-gone) over to
  …으로 가다
step up on …위로 올라가다
platform 회전목마대, 플랫폼
pretend to …인 체하다
horse 말(회전목마)
hardly 도저히 …않다
wait 기다리다
ride 타다, 탈것(놀이기구)

run(-ran-run) to …로 달려가다
hand someone money
  … 에게 돈을 건네다
jump on to … 로 뛰어오르다
actually 실제로, 사실
back 등
wow! (감탄사)와!
real 진짜의
fur 털
start 움직이다, 시작하다
suddenly 갑자기
realize 깨닫다, 알아차리다

The hungry old wolf jumped off the
Merry-Go-Round and began running off
with the first pig on his back.

 Help!! Let me off!!

 Now I've got you!

The scared little pig knew he had to do
something. So he slid off the wolf's back
and ran to find his brother. The second
pig was about to get on the Ferris Wheel
when he heard the cries of the first little
pig.

jump off 뛰어내리다
merry-go-round 회전목마
begin(-began-begun) … ing
　… 하기 시작하다
run off with …을 가지고 달아나다
help 도와 주다
let off 풀어 주다
get(-got-gotten) 잡다
scared 무서움에 질린
know(-knew-known) 알다

have(-had-had) to … 해야 한다
slide (-slid-slid) off
　… 에서 미끄러져 내리다
find 찾다
be about to 지금 막 … 하려고 하다
get on 타다
ferris wheel 회전 관람차
hear(-heard-heard) 듣다
cries 고함, 울음 소리

The hungry old wolf jumped off the Merry-Go-Round and began
running off with the first pig on his back.
굶주린 늙은 늑대는 회전목마에서 뛰어내려 등에 첫째 돼지를 업고 달아나
기 시작했습니다.

The w-w-wolf is here!! Help!

 The wolf is HERE? Hurry, get on the Ferris Wheel with me. Mister, send us to the top...QUICKLY!

When the wolf saw that the two pigs were on the Ferris Wheel, he jumped on and began climbing to the top where they were. He was getting closer and closer. But as soon as the pigs reached the bottom again, they jumped off and begged the Ferris Wheel man to help them.

here 여기에

hurry 서두르다

mister (남자의 호칭)선생님, 아저씨

send someone to the top
　…을 꼭대기로 보내다

quickly 재빨리

climb to …로 올라가다

get closer and closer
　점점 더 가까워지다

as soon as …하자마자

reach the bottom 바닥에 닿다

again 다시, 또

beg 부탁하다, 간청하다

He jumped on and began climbing to the top where they were.

늑대는 회전 관람차에 뛰어올라 돼지들이 있는 꼭대기까지 올라가기
시작했습니다.

Please mister, keep the hungry old wolf away from us!!

No problem, little pigs. I know just what to do.

The man turned the Ferris Wheel speed to turbo and gave the wolf a real ride for his money.

He isn't going to feel like eating pigs or anything else for a while.

Thanks! We won't have to worry about him now.

please 제발, 부탁이에요
keep away 가까이 못하게 하다
no problem 문제 없어
turn speed to turbo
  속도를 터보로 돌리다
give(-gave-given) 주다
real 진짜의, 진정한
for one's money 안성맞춤의

be going to …할 것이다
feel like … ing …하고 싶어하다
anything else
  그 밖에 또 무엇인가[다른]
for a while 잠깐, 잠시 동안
thank 감사하다, 고마워하다
worry about … 에 대해 걱정하다

He isn't going to feel like eating pigs or anything else for a while.
늑대는 한동안 돼지나 그 밖의 다른 것을 먹고 싶은 생각이 안 들 거야.

We won't have to worry about him now.
이제 우린 늑대에 대해 걱정할 필요가 없게 됐어.

Just then, the first little pig saw a sign pointing to the pie eating contest.

Come on, brother. This is what I came for! Where do I sign up?

The first pig entered the pie eating contest and the second pig cheered him on. The little pig ate and ate. In fact, several hours later, he was STILL eating pies.

Keep it up brother, you're winning!

just then 바로 그 때
sign 표시판, 간판
point to …을 가리키다
pie eating contest 파이 먹기 시합
come on (재촉할 때) 자, 가자구
come(-came-come) for
  …의 목적으로 오다

sign up 서명하다
enter 참여하다
cheer 응원하다, 환호하다
keep it up (지금까지처럼) 계속
  노력하다
win 이기다

This is what I came for! Where do I sign up?
이게 바로 내가 온 이유야! 어디에 서명하면 되죠?

Keep it up brother, you're winning!
형이 이기고 있어, 계속 해!

Someone else was secretly cheering the little pig on.

The more you eat, the sweeter you will taste, little piggy.

Finally, all the other contestants gave up, and the first little pig was declared the winner.

Congratulations, little pig! You are this year's Pie Eating Contest winner!! Will you say a few words?

Ugggggg!

someone else 누군가 딴 사람
secretly 비밀히, 남 몰래
sweeter (sweet의 비교급)더 달콤한
taste 맛이 나다
finally 마침내, 드디어
contestant 경쟁자

give(-gave-given) up 포기하다
declare 선언하다, 공표하다
winner 승리자
say 말하다
a few 약간의, 몇 개의
words 말, 이야기

The more you eat, the sweeter you will taste, little piggy.
아기 돼지야, 네가 많이 먹으면 먹을수록 너의 고기맛은 더 달콤해질
거란다.

Will you say a few words?   몇 말씀 하시겠어요?

Ah ha! He's too full to even talk, much less run. I'll just walk over and grab him.

Little did the wolf know, but the third little pig knew what he was up to and had a plan of his own. The wolf came out of hiding and started coming after the first and second little pigs.

Watch out! Here comes the hungry old wolf again!

What do we do now?

I don't know! There's no way I can run after eating all those pies!

I have you now, little pigs. There's no where to hide.

He's too full to even talk, much less run.
저 녀석 너무 배가 불러서 뛰는 것은 고사하고 말조차 못 하는군.

There's no way I can run after eating all those pies!
그 파이를 다 먹고 나서 뛸 수 있다는 건 말도 안 돼!

too ~ to … 너무 ~해서
　…할 수가 없다
full 배부른
even 심지어, …조차도
talk 말하다
much less …은 말할 것도 없이
just 바로, 당장
walk over …로 걸어가다
grab 붙잡다
up to …을 꾀하고
plan of one's own 자신만의 계획

come out …에서 나오다
hiding 숨은 장소
start 시작하다
come after …을 따라가다
watch out 조심하다, 주의하다
here comes someone
　누군가 이리로 오다
no way (구어)천만의 말씀,
　조금도 …않다
after …한 후에

Just then, the third little pig came to the rescue of his brothers.

 Hurry, jump in this barrel. We are going to roll you home.

What???

Just do it! We are running out of time!

So the first little pig jumped into the barrel and his brothers quickly began rolling him home with the wolf close behind them.

come 오다
rescue 구조, 구제
jump in(to) …로 뛰어들다
barrel (가운데가 불룩한)통, 맥주통
roll 굴리다
just 단지, 그저

run out of time 시간이 다
  되어 가다
begin(-began-begun) 시작하다
close 가까운
behind …의 뒤에

We are going to roll you home.
우리가 형을 집까지 굴려서 갈게.

with the wolf close behind them
늑대가 그들 뒤를 바짝 따라옴과 동시에

When they finally got home, the pigs locked all the doors and all the windows. The wolf arrived at the pigs' home moments later. He knew from past experience that he couldn't blow this house down, so he just waited outside, knowing the pigs would have to come out sooner or later.

finally 마침내, 드디어
get(-got-gotten) home
  집에 도착하다
lock 잠그다
all 모든
window 창문
arrive at …에 도착하다

moments later 잠시 후에
past experience 지난 경험
blow down 불어서 쓰러뜨리다
outside 밖에서
come out 나오다
sooner or later 조만간

He knew from past experience that he couldn't blow this house down, so he just waited outside, knowing the pigs would have to come out sooner or later. 늑대는 지난 경험으로 이 집을 불어서 쓰러뜨릴 수 없다는 걸 알았습니다. 그래서 돼지들이 조만간에 집에서 나와야 한다는 것을 알고 그저 밖에서 기다렸습니다.

103

He's STILL out there!

 What are we going to do?

 Well, I guess we should just ask him to join us for dinner.

 What?? Are you crazy?!

 Trust me. I have a plan. I've already got the pot of water boiling in the fireplace.

I guess we should just ask him to join us for dinner.
내 생각엔 우리가 늑대에게 저녁 식사를 함께 하자고 물어 봐야 할 것 같아.

I've already got the pot of water boiling in the fireplace.
난 벌써 벽난로에 끓는 물 한 단지를 준비해 놨거든.

still 여전히

out there 저 바깥에

guess …이라고 생각하다

just 그냥 한번

ask 묻다, 물어 보다

join 함께하다, 참여하다

dinner 저녁 식사

crazy 미친, 제정신이 아닌

trust 믿다, 신뢰하다

plan 계획

already 이미, 벌써

get 손에 넣다, 준비하다

pot of water 물단지

boiling 끓고 있는

fireplace 벽난로

So, the third little pig opened the door and invited the wolf for dinner.

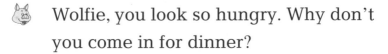 Wolfie, you look so hungry. Why don't you come in for dinner?

I would love to join you for dinner.

But when the wolf tried to enter the house, the door slammed shut.

open the door 문을 열다	join 함께하다, 참여하다
invite 초대하다, 초청하다	try to …하려고 하다
wolfie 늑대의 애칭	enter 들어가다
look …처럼 보이다	house 집
why don't you …?	slam (문 등이)쾅 닫히다
…하는 게 어때요?	shut 닫힌
would love to …하고 싶다	

Why don't you come in for dinner?
들어와서 저녁 식사 하실래요?

the door slammed shut. 문이 쾅소리를 내며 닫혔습니다.

I'm so sorry, Wolfie. The wind must have blown the door closed. Why don't you come in through the window.

So the wolf ran to the window. But just as he tried to go in, the window suddenly closed.

sorry 미안한, 후회하는	come in 들어오다
wind 바람	through …을 통하여
must have (과거 분사)…	window 창문
…했음에 틀림없다	run (-ran-run) to …로 달려가다
blow (-blew-blown) 바람이 불다	suddenly 갑자기

The wind must have blown the door closed.
바람이 불어서 문이 닫힌 게 틀림없어요.

But just as he tried to go in, 하지만 늑대가 막 들어가려고 하자,

Ooops! How clumsy of me. The window just slipped out of my hands. The chimney is the only other way into the house. But I think you're too big to fit. I'm sorry, Wolfie.

He thinks he can fool me. I'll give him a big surprise and show him I CAN fit down the chimney.

The hungry old wolf climbed up to the roof and slipped down the chimney, ready to surprise the three little pigs.

oops 이런, 아차, 앗 실례
how 너무나, 매우
clumsy 서투른, 꼴사나운
slip 미끄러지다
out of my hands 내 손에서
chimney 굴뚝
only 유일한
other way 다른 방법
into the house 집 안으로
too ~ to … 너무 ~해서 …할 수 없다

fit 꼭 맞다
fool 속이다, 놀리다
give someone a surprise
　　…를 놀라게 하다
show 보여 주다
climb up to …로 올라가다
roof 지붕
ready to 각오가 되어 있는,
　　언제든지 …하려는
surprise 놀라게 하다

Ooops! How clumsy of me. 아차! 난 정말 조심성이 없다니까.

The chimney is the only other way into the house.
굴뚝이 집 안으로 들어올 수 있는 유일한 또 다른 방법이죠.

But I think you're too big to fit.
하지만 제가 생각하기에 당신은 몸집이 너무 커서 맞지가 않을 것 같네요.

ready to surprise the three little pigs.
세 마리 돼지를 놀라게 해줄 각오를 하고서

But it was HE that was surprised. When the wolf reached the bottom, he fell right into the little pigs' cooking pot. And that was the end of the hungry old wolf. With their wolf troubles now finally behind them, you can be sure the three little pigs lived happily ever after!

reach the bottom 바닥에 닿다	trouble 근심, 걱정
fall(-fell-fallen) into	behind …의 뒤에
…으로 떨어지다	sure 확실한, 분명한
right 곧바로	live 살다
cooking pot 요리용 단지[냄비]	happily 행복하게
end 종말, 최후	ever after 이후 내내

But, it was HE that was surprised.
하지만 깜짝 놀란 것은 오히려 늑대였습니다.

With their wolf troubles now finally behind them,
마침내 이제는 늑대에 대한 걱정을 뒤로 한 채,

Comprehension

Checkup IV

I   True or False

1. The Fair was at the Village Square.
2. The third little pig wanted to buy farm supplies.
3. The wolf pretended to be a Ferris Wheel man.
4. The first little pig won the pie eating contest.
5. The wolf did not fit down the chimney.

II   Multiple Choice

1. **Why did the wolf go to the fair?**
   a. He wanted to catch the little pigs.
   b. He wanted to enter the pie eating contest.
   c. He wanted to ride the Merry-Go-Round.

2. **How did the Ferris Wheel man help the little pigs?**
   a. He gave the wolf a pie.
   b. He stopped the Ferris Wheel.
   c. He turned the Ferris Wheel speed to turbo.

정답은 p.121에

3. How long did the first little pig eat pies?

    a. He ate for several minutes.

    b. He ate for several hours.

    c. He ate for several days.

4. How did they get the first little pig home?

    a. They all ran home.

    b. They rode the Ferris Wheel home.

    c. They rolled him home in a barrel.

5. What did the third little pig put in the fireplace?

    a. He put a pan of bacon in the fireplace.

    b. He put a pot of boiling water in the fireplace.

    c. He put a pile of bricks in the fireplace.

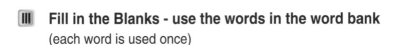

III **Fill in the Blanks - use the words in the word bank**
(each word is used once)

arrived	away	eating	guess	him
join	mister	ran	something	way

1. When they _____, they each wanted to do _____ different.

2. He _____ to the man and handed _____ the money.

3. Please _____, keep the hungry old wolf _____ from us!

4. There's no _____ I can run after _____ all those pies!

5. Well, I _____ we should just ask him to _____ us for dinner.

정답은 p.121에

IV **Draw a line to connect the words that are opposites of each other:**

A	B
Sell •	• By oneself
Remember •	• Late
Early •	• Dumb
Together •	• Forget
Smart •	• Buy

Checkup I (30~33p)

| I | 1. T | 2. F | 3. F | 4. T | 5. T |

| II | 1. b | 2. a | 3. a | 4. c | 5. c |

III
1. time, into   2. hard, new
3. build, quickly 4. wait, any
5. loves, plays

| **A** | **B** |

IV

Mother Pig — was hungry.

The first little pig — built a house out of bricks.

The second little pig — built a house out of sticks.

The third little pig — built a house out of straw.

The scary old wolf — sent her sons away.

Comprehension Checkup

Checkup II (50~53p)

I   **1.** F   **2.** F   **3.** T   **4.** T   **5.** F

II   **1.** b   **2.** c   **3.** a   **4.** c   **5.** a

III   **1.** hungry, different   **2.** mother, about
        3. safe, house   **4.** wolf, eat
        5. think, new

	A	B
IV	Little pig, little pig,	get in here.
	You will never	and the wolf went home.
	So the wolf huffed, and he puffed,	let me in please.
	The three pigs cheered,	and trick them.
	I will go back to their house tomorrow	and he blew the house down.

119

Checkup III (76~79p)

| I | 1. F | 2. F | 3. T | 4. T | 5. T |

| II | 1. c | 2. a | 3. c | 4. b | 5. a |

III 1. where, when   2. able, pig
     3. work, food   4. making, their
     5. trees, gathering

| **A** | **B** |

IV The wolf went to   •   • with me this time.
    the pigs house

    I know a really   •   • with him.
    good field

    Do you want to go   •   • with lots of carrots.

    We should have gone   •   • with a big, friendly
                                             smile.

    You have to come   •   • with me?

Comprehension Checkup

Checkup IV (114~117p)

Ⅰ **1.** T   **2.** T   **3.** F   **4.** T   **5.** F

Ⅱ **1.** a   **2.** c   **3.** b   **4.** c   **5.** b

Ⅲ **1.** arrived, something   **2.** ran, him
    3. mister, away   **4.** way, eating
    5. guess, join

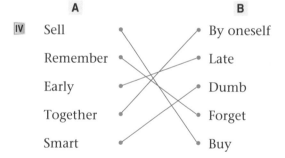

A	B
Sell	By oneself
Remember	Late
Early	Dumb
Together	Forget
Smart	Buy

Word List

다음은 이 책에 나오는 단어와 숙어를 수록한 것입니다.
* 표는 중학교 영어 교육 과정의 기본 어휘입니다.

A

a few*	97
a whole mountain of	75
actually	87
admire	27
advertisement	81
afraid*	41 / 45
after*	99
again*	91
all*	102
all by oneself	65
all right!	65
already*	65 / 105
always*	15
animal*	35
any longer	25
anyone	73
anything else	93
apple*	67
apple pie	71
arrive*	85

arrive at	102
as fast as one could	41 / 45
as soon as	91
ask*	67 / 105
at a time	85
at five o'clock	61 / 69
at that very moment	73

B

back*	87
bacon	35 / 59
bake	75
bang	41
barn	57
barrel	101
be able to	59
be about to	89
be excited about	83
be going to	45 / 71 / 93
be mad at	69
be made of	45

T

Story House
06. The Three Little Pigs 아기 돼지 삼형제

펴낸이	임 병 업
펴낸곳	(주)월드컴 에듀
등록	2000년 1월 17일
주소	강남구 언주로 118
	우성캐릭터199 2108호
전화	02)3273-4300(대표)
팩스	02)3273-4303
홈페이지	www.wcbooks.co.kr
이메일	wc4300@wcbooks.co.kr

* 본 교재는 저작권법에 의해 보호를 받는 저작물이므로
  무단전재 및 무단복제를 금합니다.